Animal Babies
A Random House PICTUREBACK®

M000098276

Baby orangutan

Wild turkeys

Animal Babies

by Harry McNaught

Random House · New York

Copyright © 1977 by Random House, Inc. All rights reserved under International and Pan-American Copyright Conventions. Published in the United States by Random House, Inc., New York, and simultaneously in Canada by Random House of Canada Limited, Toronto. Library of Congress Catalog Card Number: 76-24175. ISBN: 0-394-83570-0   Manufactured in the United States

Rabbit babies are called kits. They cannot see or hear until they are about ten days old.

A baby deer is called a fawn. The fawn's spotted back helps it hide in the shadowy forest.

Lion cubs lose their spots as they grow older.

Baby swans are called cygnets. They are covered with soft, grayish-brown feathers called down. The mother swan makes a nest of plants and soft down from her own body.

Baby ducks follow their mother
everywhere. When ducklings are only
one day old, they begin to swim.

A foal can run a few
hours after it is born.

A mother pig, called a sow,
can have as many as twenty-seven
piglets in one litter.

Both the mother and father robin
bring worms and insects for their
hungry babies to eat.

When baby alligators are ready to hatch, they make a noise inside their shells. The babies break through the shells by using a tiny tooth on their snouts.

Flamingo chicks bark like puppies when they are hungry.

South American anteaters use their long, sticky tongues for picking up ants. The baby anteater sometimes rides on its mother's back.

Bison stay together in herds. The leader of the herd helps the mothers protect their calves from enemies.

Polar bear cubs love to wrestle and climb.

Baby zebras are called colts. Their stripes help them hide in the tall grass. When a giraffe calf is born, it is almost as tall as a full-grown man.

The baby hippopotamus will not stray far from its mother.

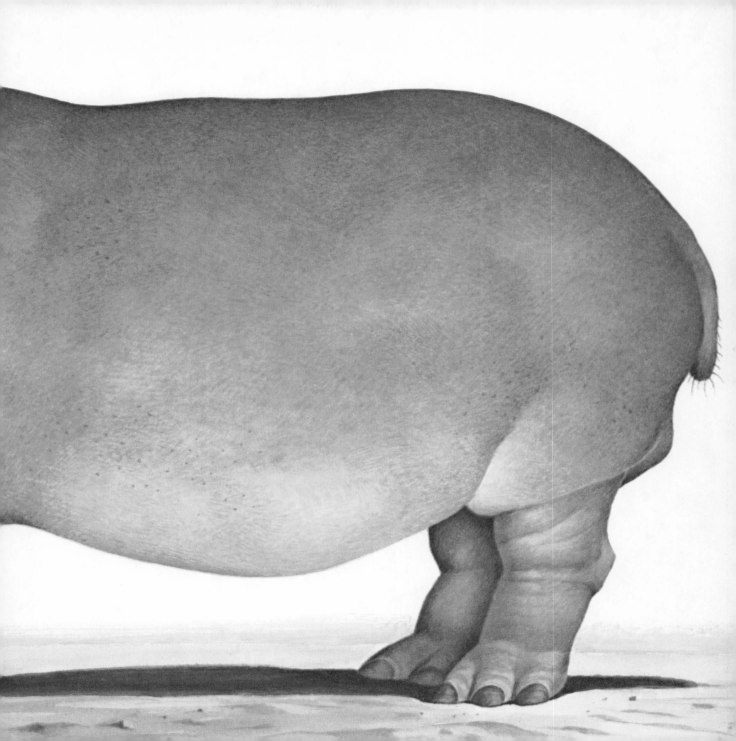

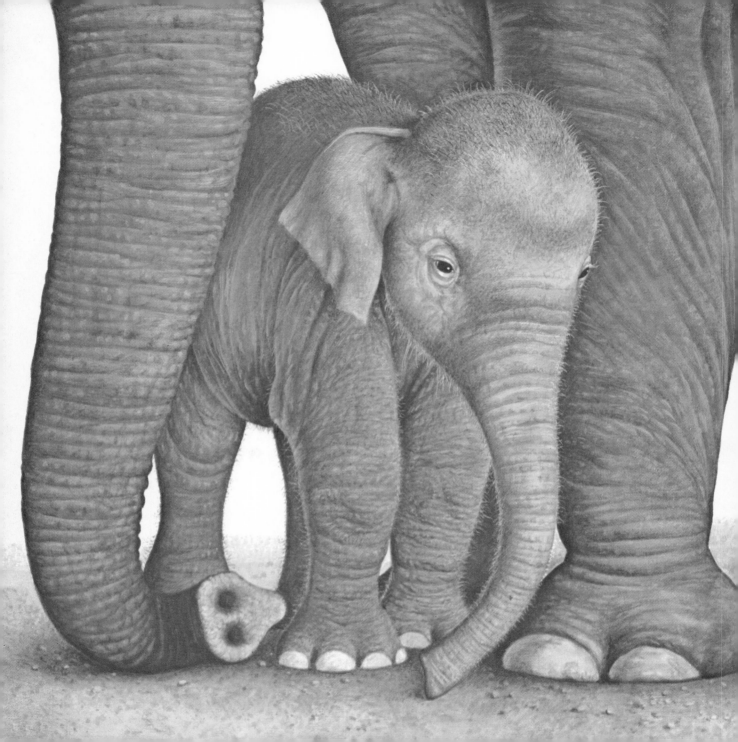

Elephant calves are playful.
They love to tease their mothers.

The baby rhinoceros begins to grow horns soon after it is born.

Penguin chicks are covered with fluffy, gray down. Parents gather round the chicks to protect them from the cold.

A baby kangaroo is called a joey.
It does not leave its mother's pouch
until it is about four months old.

The baby koala clings to its mother until it is almost as big as she is. Koalas get most of their water from the leaves of the eucalyptus tree.